DUMB AND DUMBER

JOKE BOOK

by Megan Stine

Based on the motion picture
written by Peter Farrelly &
Bennett Yellin & Bobby Farrelly

A PARACHUTE PRESS BOOK

SCHOLASTIC INC.
New York Toronto London Auckland Sydney

ISBN 0-590-59885-6

NEW LINE CINEMA PRESENTS IN ASSOCIATION WITH MOTION PICTURE CORPORATION OF AMERICA A BRAD KREVOY/STEVE STABLER/CHARLES B. WESSLER PRODUCTION A FARRELLY BROTHERS FILM JIM CARREY JEFF DANIELS "DUMB AND DUMBER" LAUREN HOLLY KAREN DUFFY AND TERI GARR EXECUTIVE PRODUCERS GERALD T. OLSON AARON MEYERSON WRITTEN BY PETER FARRELLY & BENNETT YELLIN & BOB FARRELLY PRODUCED BY CHARLES B. WESSLER, BRAD KREVOY AND STEVE STABLER DIRECTED BY PETER FARRELLY   NEW LINE CINEMA

Photo credits
Mark Fellman: p.15, p.23, p.30, p.34, p.41, p.42, p.49, p.54, p.57, p.65, and p.83.
B. Little: p.5, p.11, p.37, p.60, p.66, p.71, p.74, p.78, p.96, and all headshots throughout.

Published by Scholastic Inc.
Created by Parachute Press, Inc.

12 11 10 9 8 7 6 5 4 3 2 1   5 6 7 8 9/9 0/0
Printed in the U.S.A.
First Scholastic printing, July 1995

MOST

LIKELY

TO BE...

DUMB

Harry and Lloyd were talking about their days in school.

"When I was in high school, I ran for class president," Harry said. "I got thirty-seven out of thirty-eight votes!"

"Wow!" Lloyd said. "That's pretty good."

"Yeah," Harry agreed. "And I would have gotten even more if I'd voted for myself!"

6

"If you had six candy bars and I asked you for one, how many would you have left?" Harry asked.

"Six!" Lloyd said, smacking his lips.

"Did you have a hard time when you were in school?" Harry asked Lloyd.

"Yeah, I sure did," Lloyd said.

"Me too," Harry said. "What were your three hardest years?"

"Sixth grade!" Lloyd replied.

Harry wasn't very good in math. One day he asked Lloyd for a favor.

"Can you take the math test for me, Lloyd?" Harry said.

"No, it wouldn't be right," Lloyd said.

"I know," Harry said. "But at least you could try!"

LOST

AND

DUMBFOUNDED

A police officer pulled Lloyd over to the side of the road.

"You're in trouble, buddy," the cop said. "This is a one-way street."

"What's the problem?" Lloyd asked. "I'm only going one way!"

"Harry, I think there's something wrong with my left turn signal. Go around behind the car and tell me if it's working."

"Yeah, Lloyd, it's working . . . no, it's not . . . yeah, it's working . . . no, it's not. . ."

Lloyd and two college professors were on a trip to the Sahara Desert. They were all told that they could take only one thing with them.

The first professor said, "I'm going to take a sandwich so that, if I get hungry, I can eat."

The second professor said, "I'm going to take a jug of water. That way, if I get thirsty, I can drink."

Lloyd said, "I'm going to take a car door. That way, if it gets hot, I can roll the window down!"

Harry and Lloyd were speeding down the road. A police car pulled them over.

"You were going eighty!" the officer yelled. "Why on earth were you driving so fast?"

"We have a good reason," Lloyd explained to the cop. "Our brakes are no good — so we wanted to get there before we had an accident!"

Lloyd and Harry were driving around a mountain road. And Lloyd was driving way too fast. Harry was clinging to him for dear life.

Finally Harry couldn't take it anymore. "Slow down, Lloyd," Harry begged. "I get scared every time you go around one of these curves."

"Then just do what I do, Harry," Lloyd advised. "Close your eyes!"

On the way to the airport, Lloyd was driving a limousine really fast, and he kept turning around to talk to Mary in the backseat.

"Uh, Lloyd, could you please watch where you're going?" Mary said. "You just ran through a red light, and two cars back there crashed into each other."

"Boy, I know what you mean," Lloyd said. "There sure are a lot of bad drivers on the road!"

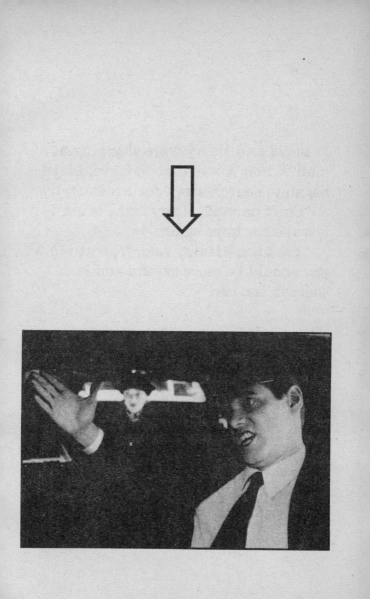

Lloyd and Harry were shopping at a mall. When it was time to leave, Lloyd began to search his pockets frantically.

"Don't be mad, Harry, but I think I lost the car keys again."

"You idiot!" Harry said. "Next time you should be more careful and lock them in the car!"

⇩

A week later, Lloyd and Harry were shopping again.

"Oh, no, Harry," Lloyd said. "I just accidentally locked the keys in the car!"

"That's really dumb," Harry said. "Now how are we going to get in?"

"Yeah," Lloyd said. "And my mom's in there too. She'll probably starve by the time I get her out!"

18

DUMB

AT

WORK

A woman was standing in her living room, talking to a friend. Every few minutes she'd walk over to the window and call out, "Green side up!"

"Why are you doing that?" the friend asked.

"I have to," the woman said, "because I have Lloyd and Harry working for me."

"What are they doing?" the friend asked.

"Planting sod!" the woman replied.

"Don't you hate going to work every day, Lloyd?" Harry asked.

"Nah," Lloyd said, "I don't mind going and I don't mind coming home. It's the part in between that I don't like!"

A health inspector walked into the restaurant where Lloyd was working as a cook.

"This restaurant is filthy!" the inspector said. "You've got too many roaches in here!"

"Well, how many are we allowed to have?" Lloyd replied.

Harry got a job where he had to dress up like a rabbit. After a few weeks his costume was looking pretty grungy.

"Harry, that bunny costume looks terrible," Lloyd said. "It's dirty, it's torn, and the tail is falling off."

"I know," Harry said. "I'm having a bad hare day!"

"Boy, you look tired," Harry said to Lloyd. "Hard day at work?"

"I'll say," Lloyd replied. "The computer went down, and I had to think all day!"

"How come we're always out of work?" Harry asked Lloyd one night at a party.

"Because we don't know how to do anything," Lloyd replied.

"You're right," Harry said. "We should learn a trade. Then we'd know what kind of work we're out of!"

Lloyd and Harry were reading the help wanted ads in the newspaper.

"Here's an ad for a waiter," Lloyd said. "But I don't want the job."

"Why not?" Harry said.

"It's too hard," Lloyd said. "You have to fill the salt shakers — and it's so hard to get the salt in through those tiny holes!"

A woman walked into a pet store where Harry was working.

"Excuse me," she said, "but could you help me out?"

"Sure," Harry said. "Just go through that door!"

A man walked up to Lloyd at the party and offered him a job.

"I'll call you tomorrow," the man said. "What's your phone number?"

"It's in the phone book," Lloyd replied.

"Okay, well what's your name?" the man asked.

"Oh, that's in the book too!" Lloyd said.

A rich man hired Lloyd as a chauffeur. One day he called Lloyd out to the garage.

"When I hired you as a chauffeur," the man said, "I told you I expected you to wash the car. But that car looks like it hasn't been washed in two months!"

"Don't look at me," Lloyd said. "I've been on the job for only two weeks!"

⟹

Harry came home one day with good news.

"I got a new job at the Burger Palace today," he told Lloyd.

"How many people work there?" Lloyd asked.

"Oh, about half of them!" Harry replied.

Harry and Lloyd went to a factory, looking for work. When they arrived, they found the workers marching up and down in front with picket signs.

"Hey, look, Harry," Lloyd said. "The factory workers are on strike for shorter hours."

"Sounds good to me," Harry said. "I've always thought that sixty minutes was too much for an hour!"

"I just applied for a job as a night watchman in a bank," Lloyd told Harry at lunch one day.

"Have you ever been a night watchman before?" Harry asked.

"No," Lloyd admitted.

"Well, what makes you think you're qualified?" Harry asked.

"Because," Lloyd said, "the slightest noise and I'm awake."

OH,

DUMBWAITER!

"What's the difference between a ham and cheese sandwich and a bag of manure?" Lloyd asked Harry.

"I don't know," Harry said.

"Oh, yeah?" Lloyd said. "Well, I'll never send you out to buy lunch!"

One night Lloyd offered to make dinner.

"I know how to cook only two things: meat loaf and scrambled eggs," Lloyd said.

"Fine," Harry said. "Which one is this?"

⬇

During dinner at a fancy restaurant, Harry kept reaching across the table for the salt.

"Harry," Lloyd whispered. "Don't keep reaching for things. Don't you have a tongue?"

"Sure," Harry replied, "but my arm is longer!"

Harry and Lloyd stopped at a road-side restaurant. When the waitress brought their lunch, Lloyd looked at his food and started to gag.

"Excuse me, miss," Lloyd said, "but this hamburger isn't fit for a pig!"

"Okay," the waitress said. "I'll take it back and bring you one that is!"

Harry and Lloyd walked into a coffee shop and sat down at the counter.

"I'll have a cup of coffee with cream and sugar," Harry said.

"Me too," Lloyd said. "And make sure the cup is clean."

A minute later the waitress came back. "Here you go," she said. "But which one of you gets the clean cup?"

"Hey, Lloyd, can you name the four seasons?"

"Sure, Harry. Salt, pepper, vinegar, and mustard."

$\Rightarrow$

Lloyd walked into a pizza shop to pick up a pizza he had ordered.

"Do you want this pizza cut into six or eight pieces?" the man behind the counter asked.

"Only six," Lloyd said. "I don't think I can eat eight!"

DUMBSTRUCK!

Lloyd had been in love with Mary from the first moment he saw her. Finally, they were alone together.

"Mary, I'm in love with you," Lloyd said. "And I want you to tell me the truth. What are the chances of a girl like you ending up with a guy like me?"

"Well, Lloyd," she said gently. "Not good."

"Come on, tell me straight," Lloyd said. "You mean not good, like one in a hundred?"

"No," Mary said, shaking her head. "I'd say more like one in a million."

Lloyd paused and swallowed hard. "Okay," he said, "so you're telling me there's a chance!"

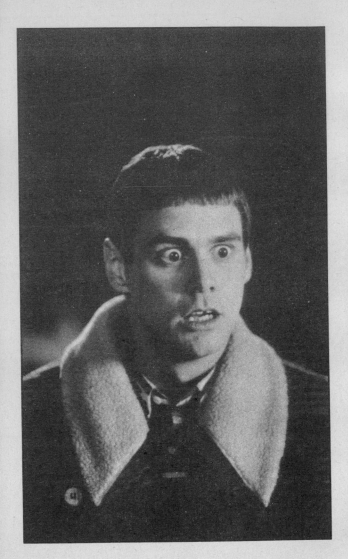

Lloyd was so in love, he decided to propose marriage. He went to Mary's father to ask permission to marry his daughter. But when he got there, Lloyd was so tongue-tied, he didn't know what to say. Finally Mary's father spoke up.

"Well, Lloyd," Mr. Swanson said. "Have you come to ask for my daughter's hand?"

"No way!" Lloyd replied. "I want the whole girl or it's no deal!"

Lloyd had been in love with Mary for a long time. But one day he changed his mind.

"I don't like Mary anymore," Lloyd told Harry.

"Why not?" Harry asked.

"Because she said, 'A penny for your thoughts,'" Lloyd explained. "So I told her what I was thinking — and she asked for her money back!"

Lloyd and Harry were talking about marriage.

"Boy, I've had a lot of great girl-friends," Lloyd said, bragging. "A lot of them sure are going to be miserable when I get married."

"Really?" Harry said. "How many of them are you going to marry!"

RELATIVELY

DUMB

Hey, Harry! My sister's having a baby!

Lloyd was bragging about his family to Harry.

"My sister's baby is a year old, and he's been walking ever since he was eight months!" Lloyd said.

"Boy," Harry said, "he must be really tired!"

Harry's family was nothing to brag about. One day he told Lloyd, "I had to put my brother in a rehab clinic."

"Really? How come?" Lloyd asked.

"Because he was hooked on phonics!" Harry replied.

Congratulations! But are you going to be an uncle or an aunt?

Harry walked out of a drugstore with a small bag in his hand.

"I just got a pack of gum for my sister," Harry said.

"Sounds like a good swap to me!" Lloyd replied.

Lloyd went to visit his grandmother.

"Hello, Lloyd," his grandmother said. "Will you join me in a cup of tea?"

"Oh, I don't know," Lloyd said. "I don't think there's room in there for both of us!"

DOGGONE

DUMB

$\Rightarrow$

"I got a new dog," Harry told Lloyd. "Why don't you come over and see him?"

"Does he bite?" Lloyd asked.

"I don't know," Harry said. "That's what I want to find out!"

"I got a new dog," Harry said.

"Spitz?" Lloyd asked.

"No, but he drools a lot," Harry replied.

"I got a new dog," Harry said.

"Boxer?" Lloyd asked.

"No, I let her run free," Harry replied.

"I got a new dog," Harry said.

"Pinscher?" Lloyd asked.

"No, but I scold her when she does something bad," Harry said.

What's the difference between Harry and a stray dog?

There are fewer fleas on the dog!

HARRY

IS SO

DUMB...

Harry is so dumb . . .

. . . that he has a bumper sticker that says, "Honk if you love peace and quiet."

. . . that he stayed up all night studying for his blood test!

. . . that he thinks water skis are what you use when you go to Aspen and it's raining!

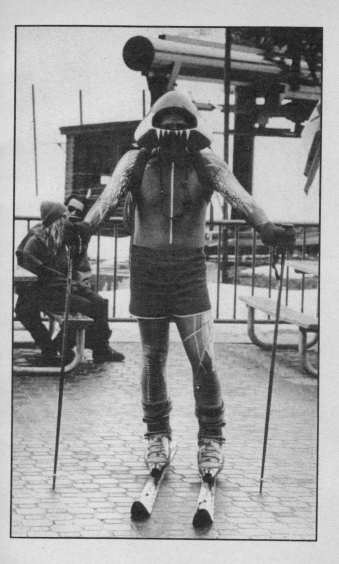

Harry is so dumb . . .

. . . that he needs a recipe to make ice cubes!

. . . that he won't use a rowing machine because he's afraid of the water!

LLOYD

IS SO

DUMB...

Lloyd is so dumb . . .

. . . that he doesn't know how many cans of soda come in a six-pack!

. . . that he wears a bathing suit to the pool hall.

Lloyd is so dumb . . .

. . . that he thinks caramel corn is a vegetable!

. . . that he stares at the mirror with his eyes shut to see what he looks like when he's asleep.

. . . that it takes him two hours to watch *60 Minutes.*

DOWN

IN

THE

DUMBPS!

"Can you drive me to the vet, Harry?"
Lloyd asked.

"What for?" Harry said.

"My canine teeth hurt!"

Lloyd walked into the doctor's office.

"Hi, Lloyd," the doctor said. "I haven't
seen you for a long time."

"I know," Lloyd replied. "That's
because I've been sick!"

When Lloyd got home from the doctor, he decided to give Harry some advice.

"You ought to go to my doctor," Lloyd said.

"Why?" Harry asked. "There's nothing wrong with me."

"Yeah," Lloyd agreed. "But my doctor's so good, he'll find something!"

Lloyd walked into his psychiatrist's office.

"Hello, Lloyd," the doctor said. "How are you doing with that memory problem you told me about?"

"What memory problem?" Lloyd replied.

HOW

DUMB

CAN

YOU

GET?

⇨

How many dumb guys does it take to change a light bulb?

Five. One to stand there and hold the bulb — and the other four to turn the ladder!

How many dumb guys does it take to mop a floor?

No one knows — they've never done it.

How can you tell when Lloyd and Harry have been using the computer?

There's White-Out on the screen.

If Harry, Lloyd, and Mary are on the Empire State Building and they all jump at the same time, who will hit the ground first?

Mary — because Harry and Lloyd would both have to stop and ask for directions to the bottom!

Lloyd went to New York on vacation and he was telling Harry about it.

"Guess what I saw?" Lloyd said. "A skyscraper."

"Really?" Harry said. "How did it work?"

Harry and Lloyd were sitting in their living room.

"Answer the phone," Harry said.

"But it's not ringing," Lloyd said.

"I know," Harry agreed. "But I'm tired of you always leaving everything till the last minute!"

"Why are you scratching yourself, Lloyd?" Harry asked.

"Because no one else knows where I itch!" Lloyd replied.

"Hey, Lloyd! Why did you bring your bowling ball into the bathroom?" Harry asked.

"Because I wanted to see the toilet bowl!"

"When's your birthday, Lloyd?" Harry asked.

"June 19."

"What year?"

"Every year," Lloyd replied.

Why didn't anyone buy the dictionary that Lloyd wrote?

Because it wasn't in alphabetical order!

What happens when Harry and Lloyd forget to pay their garbage bill?

They stop delivery!

"How do you spell Mississippi?" Harry asked.

"Which one?" Lloyd replied. "The river or the state?"

When Lloyd was in school he was pretty dumb. But he had an even dumber friend named Cody. One day he saw Cody standing by the drink machine. Cody kept putting a five-dollar bill into the machine, but the machine just kept spitting it out each time.

"Hey, Cody," Lloyd said. "Why do you keep putting that five-dollar bill into the drink machine? It doesn't take fives."

Just then Cody put the five-dollar bill in one more time. This time it didn't come back out.

"Ha ha," Lloyd said. "The machine just ate your five — and it didn't even give you a drink!"

"See?" Cody said. "I told you it would take my five!"

"When I was a kid," Lloyd said, "I used to hate my lunch. Every day it was the same thing — peanut butter and jelly. Every day — peanut butter and jelly — for six years. I got sick of it."

"But, Lloyd," Harry said. "Why didn't you ask your mom to make you something different?"

"Why should I do that?" Lloyd said. "I made my own lunch!"

"Did you give the fish fresh water today?" Harry asked Lloyd.

"Naw," Lloyd replied. "They haven't finished what I gave them yesterday!"

Lloyd and Harry went to the shopping mall, and they were in a hurry.

"Don't get on that escalator," Lloyd said.

"Why not?" Harry asked.

"Because I'm afraid the power will go off," Lloyd said.

"Oh, yeah," Harry agreed. "And then we'd be stuck there all day!"

At the mall Harry and Lloyd walked into a clothing store.

"Would you like to try on that suit in the window?" the clerk asked Lloyd.

"Yes, please," Lloyd replied. "But could I use the dressing room like everyone else?"

"Lloyd, do you realize that most people use only a quarter of their brain?" Harry said.

"Yeah," Lloyd said. "I wonder what they do with the other quarter?"

Lloyd and two wise men were standing on a thin ledge at the edge of a cliff and there was only one way out — down. Suddenly a genie appeared and said, "Jump."

"Huh?" Lloyd said.

"Jump," the genie said. "You'll be fine. Just remember that whatever word you say as you jump — that's the thing you'll become."

So the first wise man jumped off the cliff and said, "Eagle." And he flew off into the sky.

The second wise man jumped and said, "Hawk." Then he, too, flew off into the sky.

"Your turn," the genie said to Lloyd.

"Holy cow!" Lloyd cried as he jumped off the edge of the cliff.

Harry was on an airplane for the first time. After about an hour, he motioned to one of the flight attendants to come over.

"Excuse me, miss," Harry said, "but could you tell the pilot to stop turning on the seat belt sign?"

"Why?" the flight attendant asked.

"Because every time he does, the ride gets bumpy!" Harry exclaimed.

"Hey, Harry," Lloyd said. "How did you break your finger?"

"I didn't," Harry replied. "Some guy punched me in the nose!"

Harry went to the circus, but he came home disappointed.

"The knife thrower was really lame," Harry complained.

"Why?" Lloyd asked.

"Oh, man, you should have seen it," Harry said. "He threw about fifty knives at this girl — and he didn't hit her once!"

Harry was going horseback riding, and Lloyd was watching him get ready.

"Hey, Harry," Lloyd said. "You're putting that saddle on that horse backward."

"How do you know?" Harry said. "You don't know which way I'm going!"

Lloyd and Harry walked into a clothing store.

"Excuse me, sir," Lloyd said, "but I want to return this necktie."

"What's wrong with it?" the salesman asked.

"It's too tight!" Lloyd replied.

One day Lloyd and Harry rented a boat to go fishing. As soon as they got to the middle of the lake, the fish started biting like crazy. They both caught so many fish, they could hardly fit them in the boat.

"Let's take these fish home," Harry said. "And then let's come back to this exact same spot. It's terrific!"

"Okay," Lloyd agreed. "But what if we can't find the spot?"

"We'll mark it," Harry said proudly. Then he pulled out a big black marker and drew an X on the floor of the boat.

"Hey — smart move," Lloyd said. "But there's only one problem."

"What?" Harry asked.

"What if we don't get the same boat tomorrow?" Lloyd said.

REAL

NO-BRAINERS!

$\Longrightarrow$

⇩

Lloyd got arrested for speeding and went to traffic court.

"Order in the court!" the judge yelled.

"Okay," Lloyd said. "I'll have a ham sandwich!"

"Boy, I'm glad I wasn't born in France," Lloyd said to Harry one day.

"How come?" Harry said.

"Because I'd never understand anyone," Lloyd said. "I don't speak French!"

Oh, no. My parakeet Petey is dead!
Oh, man. What happened?
His head fell off.
Yeah, well, he was pretty old.

"Harry, that's the fifth movie ticket you've bought in ten minutes," Lloyd said.

"I know," Harry said. "But there's a guy in there who keeps tearing them up!"

Harry and Lloyd were walking along in the park.

"Look," Lloyd said. "A dead bird."

"Where?" Harry asked, looking up in the sky.

"Hey, Harry," Lloyd said. "Why did the chicken cross the road?"

"Duh . . . why?" Harry said.

"To get the Japanese newspaper," Lloyd said. "Get it?"

"No," Harry said.

"Me neither," Lloyd said. "I get *The New York Times.*"

"Lloyd, you're supposed to be the goalie," Harry complained during a soccer game. "Why didn't you stop the ball?"

"I thought that's what the nets were for!" Lloyd replied.

"What do George Washington, Abraham Lincoln, and Martin Luther King, Jr. have in common?" Lloyd asked Harry.

"I don't know," Harry said. "What?"

"They were all born on holidays!" Lloyd said.

Harry and Lloyd were camping one time. As soon as Harry started a fire, his pant leg caught on fire. Lloyd didn't seem to notice.

"Lloyd! Lloyd! My leg's on fire!" Harry shouted.

"What should I do?" Lloyd asked.

"Don't just stand there," Harry said. "Quick! Get the marshmallows!"

Lloyd really wanted to go on vacation. "I'm sick of this place," he said to Harry. "I wish we could just get out of here and go to China."

"Nah," Harry said. "We can't go all the way to China. But maybe we could go to the moon."

"Huh?" Lloyd said.

"Well, the moon's a lot closer, isn't it?" Harry said.

"Duh . . . I'm not sure," Lloyd said. "Is it?"

"Sure! I mean, we can see the moon, can't we, Lloyd? But we can't see China!"

⇩

One day Harry walked into the house and found Lloyd sitting at his desk.

"What are you doing?" Harry asked.

"I'm writing a letter to myself," Lloyd answered.

"What does it say?" Harry asked.

"How would I know? I won't get it until tomorrow!"

Harry ran out of the house early one morning.

"Am I too late for the garbage?" he called to the truck.

"No, buddy," the garbage collector called back. "Hop right in!"

Lloyd was trying to make a cake for Harry's birthday.

"This recipe is stupid," Lloyd said.

"How come?" Harry asked.

"Because it says to separate two eggs," Lloyd replied. "But it doesn't say how far!"

Lloyd woke up one morning with a huge smile on his face.

"You look happy," Harry said to him.

"I am," Lloyd said, "because today is Sunday — my favorite day of the week."

"How come?" Harry asked.

"Because every time I go to church," Lloyd said, "some guy hands me a whole plateful of money!"

Why did Harry put his pet in the Xerox machine?

He wanted to have a copycat.

What do you need when you have Harry and Lloyd up to their necks in wet cement?

More cement.

Did you hear what happened when Harry and Lloyd climbed Mt. Everest?

They reached the height of stupidity!